the thing about lovers

the thing about lovers

amber powers

for alex

stay crispy

words written all over my body

feelings I cannot hide

they tell the story of

our love,

my loss,

and the truth of how much

love

really costs.

the love

tangled raindrops

dim light fills the room
the color of our bodies subdued
my arms around you
a constant reminder of the truth

a storm raging outside,
the sound of raindrops pouring
lightning streaks across the sky
and we are feeling divine

lazy afternoon, rainy day,
on the bed we lay,
your heartbeat under my ear
every kiss, the most sincere

tangled in each other
tangled in the sheets,
we lie silently and listen to the thunder
and each other breathe

prelude

the last time that we said goodbye
it was the way you looked into my eyes
that made me realize that there was
a glimmer, a sliver
a crazy chance
no, we could never make this last
I jumped too soon, I fell too fast,
intent on not letting you become my past.
too soon after the fall
to tell where this could go at all
still the prelude to speaking the truth,
making that first move,
and then the fire of love will blaze
growing in size and strength in every which way,
until that crazy chance we finally take.

for you

for you,
my affection I can never make known
so I'll wallow silently
as I long to put my head next to your throat.
I'll watch you move through life
next to you, as your friend,
and when you find a girl,
to not be hurt, I'll pretend
and when we laugh and joke as friends,
know I entrust you with my secrets
and hidden words.
they are not for everyone to hear
for if everyone were to be told,
what a grand spectacle they'd make!
two friends, and lovers of such an age.
as seasons change and my feelings grow,
more suppressed than they'd ever know,
your eyes warm pools of brilliant blues
a gesture exchanged between me and you,
I find you know and I do too
the affection for you that can never be known.

a young love

your arms twisted around my waist
and for once I can think straight
the way our bodies fit against each other
so natural, so right
I spin in your arms
where I belong
as the band starts to play our song
our lips connected, our intimacy bared
I want the world to know you are mine
and I am not going to share
your hands on my waist
my lips at your ear
an exchange of private words
that make your lips curl up,
under that curly hair.

you, start

when it comes to you
I have no idea where to start,
and you have no idea
the place you hold in my heart.
close friends, but that's not enough for me,
I need you as close as you can be.
and when you beckon me closer,
a thrill in my heart,
I know that's not what you mean,
but it's a start.

wink

this moment is ours
to talk we are too far
but you tell me all I need to know
when you close one eye really slow.
you set a fire in my heart
with that loving silent remark.

a remark only meant for me to see,
to convey your love in one wink.
if another were to have seen
it would claim you for me.

letter from eric

I see you there, seventeen, young
when you were ten, you knew who I was
now you take no note
of me trying to work up the nerve

but there! I finally did it, crossed that curve
and now we enter unexplored land
with dangers we must swerve, hand in hand,
we can do it, I swear we can!

I've loved you since we were young,
I sang for you,
you finally heard my song.
hand in hand forever is how we belong.

your lips, my lips

you call out to me
my name a beautiful melody
when formed by your lips
lips that I dare not admit
that those I dream to kiss.
lips that frame a smile so bright,
a smile that made my night.
when you are near everything feels right.
I feel your eyes observe me as I walk,
to you only I want to talk,
to run and jump and scream,
to do all these crazy things!
your eyes with layers of meaning,
tell me you want my lips, too.

play with fire

everyone warned me about you
I thought I could play with fire

at first it felt good
and then came the hurt

as your fire kissed my skin
I thought how good it feels to sin

and now I'm throbbing red and burnt,
you were such a sweet hurt

your demons

your demons, they look like me
they look you in the eyes and laughingly tease
but darling I am begging you please
one more time to please the angel in me

lovely

as I see you waiting there,
battered and bruised,
and not a single prayer.
can I tell you all the things you do to me?
all the lovely things you do?

how beautiful that
someone like you
manages to love me
when I can't even be bothered
to love myself.

daughter

I've never wanted children but –
you say the word *daughter*
and my stomach melts to my toes
I wonder how many daughters you will have
I wonder if I may be so lucky
so as to give them to you

recite me

I was damned to love you
ever since that night
you trailed kisses down my spine
only coming up for air to recite
one of my poetic lines.

he loves me so

I open my eyes
lazily greet a new day
seeing him there
my troubles fade away
his kiss is all it takes
to bring a smile to my face
a best friend and a lover
he is one and the same
he holds me close
he dries my tears
courageously dashes all my fears
kills the spiders
plays guitar
I lie on his chest and listen to his heart
alex, my love,
my teammate for life,
I accept your proposal
and look forward
to being your wife.

wind

I found myself
so very jealous of the wind,
the way she ran her fingers
through your hair,
& brushed her soft lips
against your cheek.

challenge

he smiles at me
shakes his head
and smirks about how I'm
so difficult.
the truth is
I'm a challenge,
and he gets high
on solving me.

"I love you more"

"I love you

but I love myself more.
I have to let you go,
even though losing you will
damn near destroy me."

"then go, my love.
for I love you more
than myself.
and though losing you
will most definitely
destroy me completely,
I will always
love you more
and more
and more."

look for me in the stillness

look for me in the *s t i l l n e s s*
love,
look for me in the quiet
of your heart,
curled up at the corner
reading, waiting for you,
love in my heart
and more than ready
to recite my
love you mores.

purple is the sky

you get me high
like acid dreams
everything is
brighter
and I can
pretend life is
a better reality
and you
let go
inside me
purple is the sky
as I erupt
around you

all the shaky sounds

all the shaky sounds
my body makes
as he moves above me
making me come and quake

all the shaky sounds
our hearts make
as we try to force forever
into a relationship already teetering

daisies in winter

fight, fight
apparently our new
relationship mantra
but there are still days
you smile at me warmly,
we laugh like we are
still carefree
you tell me you love me
and I almost believe it.
these are daises
in a long cold winter,
hope that soon we will
thaw and become
blossoming spring.

the anatomy of a wish

may he come home safely.
may he realize how special this is.
may he right his wrongs before they destroy us.
may he be my husband.
this is the anatomy of
all my wishes:
that we are together
& we are happy.

all the good things

feeling your love
is magic,
stars,
wild heartbeats,
butterflies &
summer sundays.

sex, cigarettes, halsey

I lost my virginity
listening to halsey
croon about being blue
and yet being grey
while the shower cleansed
our sin
even as it was
happening
and our still-lit cigarette
burned a hole
in a towel on the floor,
forgotten.

faith

I have faith
and you think
the only thing
that means
anything
is us.

-it's kind of the same thing, isn't it?

on my way

would you wait for me one day,
kiss me as I get off the train?
would you take me in your arms,
and tell me *I'm glad you're around?*
would we have to stop so often so
we could kiss, a smile on our lips?

I'm on my way
to you
I'm closer every day
but I have to know that
you're on the other side
waiting
to see my smile

please tell me
you're out there waiting,
because if you're not
then I'll be broken

I've given everything to you,
you are my only truth.

tell me I'm not on my way
to goodbye
I'm not coming all this way

36

so I can cry
tell me I'm on my way
to our new life

I've bought my ticket,
I'm on my way,
I can't wait to
get off this train.

you're on the other side
waiting
to see my smile.

you are my poetry
and I am your poet

-it means something different to everyone

room 750

it was beyond me –
　　　how three and a half years
　　　could come crashing
　　　downdowndown

how I could invite you up
　　　to room 750
　　　a spontaneous decision
　　　an attempt

to rekindle love
　　　on a hotel bed when you didn't
　　　know I was planning to leave
　　　every moment burned into memory

and as we sit in the tub
　　　making out while it fills up
　　　kiss me a little longer, harder
　　　for it is the beginning of the end

green & blue

the moment that my eyes
laid upon your face
I knew right then that I
would never be the same

you lit a fire inside
as you painted my dreams
into the sky

all fears left behind
this will be my last ride,
no other could ever satisfy
from this affair, I shall not hide.

frozen in time, black & white
within me this picture
shall reside
a frozen life, completely mine

my heart a canvas
for what you feel inside
these painted dreams,
light up my sky at night

greens and blue, vibrant hues
the colors of eyes belonging
to me and you

green, the color of new life, new love
blue, the color of sadness and strife,
when you need to rise above
and make a new life

this life green gave to blue
breathed in her mouth
and whispered
"here, I'll save you"

drunk on each other's love,
they always felt above.

they made each other strong,
without a doubt,
two is better than one
and so are the words
"I love you."

secret

can I tell
you a
secret?

you're the best thing
to happen to me
and we both know
I'm leaving.

I tried to write about something else,
anything else . . .

all that there is
is you.

you're home

standing this close to you
I feel like a string has tethered us together
would you mind if closer to you I moved?
that glint in your eye, is it just for me?
I need to remember every word you speak.
I ache to hold your hand,
to erase the space between us.
your eyes, bold, lock onto mine
and they won't let go.
suddenly
you are my home.

reassurance

seeing you is like coming home
all the good things I've ever known
the world around me tumbles to the side
but you reach out, and set it right
scared, unsure, as I walk forward
you wink one eye
and everything is fine.

I don't think I can ever stop writing about you.

choosing you

my dearest one,
forever and every day
I'll be choosing you.
choosing to sleep by your side,
though you may steal the sheets
choosing to forgive you,
no matter who is in the wrong
choosing to bear every burden with you
because from you I draw my strength.
you see, my dear,
it will always be you for me.
just tell me my love
if you will always choose me.

you & her, him & I

looking out the window on the drive home
lights of beauty flash by me
and when I think of beauty, I think of you.
to be honest, I've thought of you all night
even though it should have been him,
it's always been him.
I wanted you there with me tonight.
I want you with me, here, now.
but you're with her, god, you're always with her.
I'm surprised to find
water drops on my shoulder
that came from my eyes.
I didn't want to cry, no, not tonight.
I've already done this a thousand times
and that stupid hope is what keeps me alive
thinking that maybe you could be mine
if you're with her
thinking of me
being with him
thinking of you
being with me.

you are the love of my life but this is broken.

pink

pink,
the color of the ink
I used to write your name
on that envelope

pink,
the color of my cheeks
and my puffy lips
as we kiss and kiss

pink,
the color of my beating heart
as I rip it out and hand it to you,
dripping on the snow

world of chances

if I show you what I'd do for you, my love
would that make you stay?
or am I simply another girl
from whom you'll walk away?
if I leave my friends for you
would you fill that void?
would you be a listener
and my partner in crime?
please accept my goofy side,
smile, and say you'll love me forever,
because you are here to stay.
if I leave my family for you, love
would you be worth the wait?
the wait to see a diamond on my finger
and someone to call my mate.
see all these things I've done for you
and would gladly do again
I've changed my life to be with you,
and I will love you until the end.
but, my darling, forever I'll wonder
if you would've done the same.
it's too late now; I suppose I'll never know
but now that you have me,
don't let me go.
because I have a world of chances for you
but even those, you're burning through.

I gave the best bits of my soul to you.

beginning
of
december
wind
whipping
my
hair
and
confusing
my
thoughts
of
you
this
night

hardwood oceans between lovers

these hardwood oceans
you always swam to me
have become dark waters
leaving no survivors.
they always told us
not to give heartbreak
a space to wiggle in
but I suppose
we weren't listening.
so you take your rest
in that room, love,
and I'll be in our bedroom.
these hardwood oceans
between lovers
become darker each night.

no one arrived

I had a dream
it was our wedding
but no one arrived
because they knew
what a sham it all was
how you entirely
destroyed us
and I stayed because
I always loved you
more than you deserved,
anyway.

the loss

I can hear you ticking

I can hear you ticking
like a clock
I can predict you like
clockwork
you're waiting
waiting
to break me down
because you know how to
time
me
so I am powerless
I can hear you ticking
like a bomb
so fucking
unpredictable.

lake michigan

they say the person you think of when you're by the ocean – that's who you love. and I know a lake is different than an ocean. but we live 2,599 miles from the atlantic and I've never even been close to it. but this lake – this lake I've waded into my entire life – it's still pretty magnificent. and with this skyline and this sunny day, I can't help but want you here with me. except, I want you with me most places. all places. when you sailed over the blue, did you want me with you? did you think of how the blue matched my eyes? how you could drown in both? a lake is different than an ocean.

again

I love you
again

you kiss me
again

I lose you
again

you'll miss me
again

I keep losing you
before I even
have you

-promise me I eventually get to keep you

colby

eighteen, today,
you would be.
our hearts
still filled
with vacancy.
you were always
the older one
that I looked
up to, but as of
today I've outlived you.
and I've only
just turned sixteen.
I still cry
for you,
and the things
you never got
to do.

this room

six months ago, you and I sat in this room
and in that moment we knew
everything would soon change
no, nothing ever stays the same

and now here I am again
remembering our memories, my friend
tears sting my eyes
but, here, I refuse to cry

refuse to spoil the times
we sat here and stared
refuse to spoil the things
we silently shared

so exactly the same
but so painfully different
everything is exactly as I remembered
but without you in it

written all over my body

foggy and unclean,
all I want to do is scream.
for no reason, with no rhyme,
you left me here to die.

the persistence of memory haunts me,
like a thief it steals my sleep
and I can't remember what it's like to be happy,
the way we used to be.

when you slipped your hand into mine,
you could read the smile dancing on my lips,
and our passionate whispers were like a
symphony,
when all you needed was me.

the painful memories give birth to a feeling of
loss,
a hole in my chest; a missing heart that is lost,
a gut-wrenching sadness that leaves me gasping.

no longer thirsting for sleep,
but for us together.
you carved my heart in two,
and I stayed up, cursing you.

I pull my hands through my hair over and over,
hoping this isn't really our closure.
black tears run down from my eyes,
staining the bed in which I lie.

now the pain is written on my body –
not through cuts or scrapes,
from ink – my own therapy.

fake tattoos, black and blue,
the ink decorates my body,
an easy way to change me
and still remember you.

whether it's hidden with clothes or on display,
all these symbols point to you,
a way to remember us two.

the elaborate designs
remind me of a time when you were mine
say it's a way to get over you,
but only I know the truth:

I keep writing these everyday to remind me
how vulnerable I was, but how I still felt safe,
to remind me of how I felt when I saw your face.

this is me keeping our memories alive,
written all over my body.

all that I have will fade

all that I have are memories of him
that time will steal away
all I have is that last look he gave
that is already beginning to fade.
I dreamed a thousand memories
were ours to make
but you abandoned the one place
we found each other
before I had a chance to say *stay*
but now I cannot remember you the same.
I don't know if I'll ever see you again
and this isn't the happy end
we could have had.
I recall your smile too many times a day,
desperate not to let it fade
but I know the day will come
when I sit, numb, realizing
I cannot reconstruct your face.

the scars you leave

I feel like a fool
for letting you play me
I should have realized
this was the stuff of make believe.

I fell in maddest,
purest, most passionate
form of love with you.

and still you didn't think I deserved to know the
truth.

and though you destroyed,
crushed, and ruined me,
I refuse to let my anger at you eat me.

I'll hide these scars deep down inside of me,
I'll try to be the smiling
girl everyone knows, naïve,
I'll do such a good job, I'll even convince me.

but deep down you're there
an angry red slash

throbbing with your memory
and aching with the sound of your voice.

when I smile at you,
it is not because you were once mine.

I am happy.
I will not let you take that from me.
but the truth is
you left the angriest scar
and you cut too deep.

I'm still not sure
what's even left of me.

deathblow

every kiss
burns

with the
thought

of what
you

did to
her

a painting in vengeance

my ruby red lipstick
decorates his neck
and his chest
and his hip bone
and his . . .
and when we are done
I'm smiling wide
he is my
painting in vengeance
and I am a
cheating bride

marred

this image of you
it owns my heart
and I can't think what would happen
if it were to tear apart;
if you weren't this person
that I want to think you are.

this image of you
has oh so many vibrant hues
but maybe reality is
they are more subdued.
scared to get to know you
scared that what I think you are
isn't at all true

then this perfect image,
this perfect you,
would be irrevocably ruined
and my heart would split in two.
this once perfect picture
marred forever,
messy black ink
and the scars I will keep
and I will remember that perfect
isn't you.

bleed ink

as I bleed ink onto the page,
our story pours out of me.
the tender rage, the fire,
the destruction,
and how loving you
ruined me.

late night vices

18 and a runaway
from a tight knit family
you taught me all your
late night vices
to help me cope.

we smoked pot
to help with the sleeplessness
and migraines
from how much
I missed them.

we got drunk
on red wine
because we felt it
the fastest
and it blurred
reality.

we fucked till we knew
we'd be sore the next day
so we didn't feel so
goddamn alone
and like we had
a fighting chance.

of all my
late night vices,
my favorite was you.

on her, on her, on her

as I stare out our window
cold cup of coffee in my hands
and you asleep in the other room,
I think about all the things you took from me
and I let you, because I thought that was
what love was.

and now I want it all back.
now you don't kiss me the same,
not with the passion we once had.
and 5 months in, you told me you'd marry me.

and your ring is on my finger
but last night you were kissing her.
and three months ago, it was a different girl.
and now your phone comes to life, a new name,
now one I don't even recognize.

and I wonder when I stopped being enough,
when I left family, I left friends,
to be here with you.
family and friends who told me this is exactly
what you'd do.
but I defended you,
because our love was so, so true.
to the idea of commitment, you were too new.

you didn't realize what it meant,
or didn't want to.
even though day after day after other woman,
I kept choosing you.

and you can say you've changed,
you can talk all day, defend your name.
but every time I close my eyes,
I see your lips on her, on her, on her & on her.
maybe you've changed but so have I.
and now that you've figured it out,
I'm saying goodbye.

regret

as I lay here
wallowing in my regrets
each one of which
orbit around you,
I curse my 18-year-old self
for thinking this is what love was,
although I really thought
this was it.

but it's you, you, you
at the center of each regret.
I let my mind wander yet.
I wonder if I can truly blame you
because despite everything,
you did love me well for a time.
you showed me all I wanted.
and then, all I didn't.

warm words, cold silence

I wanted to wrap myself up in his words
to find a home in the soft exhale
of everything he spoke
he said the word *love*
and the way it rolled off his tongue,
it was made for me.
and so I crawled inside, stretched out lazily
laid down inside it, and reveled in how it felt.
yes, this would be my home.
I love you
I repeated, and waited for him to respond
longed to wrap those words around my neck
to keep me warm,
but his silence was punishing.
I longed for him to relieve this pain
but he turned away,
leaving my heart and neck exposed
in this blizzard of cold.

chain smoking

c h a i n
s m o k i n g
you passed my love
right back to me
matching me
equally
your racing heartbeat
matched mine
your breath heavy
on my neck
you passed my love
back to me
c h a i n
s m o k i n g

beautiful in heartbreak

I am not a writer,
but I will paint all the words on you
and then kiss away the painful ones
so that even in heartbreak
you are beautiful.

the thing about lovers

that's the thing about lovers.
they take up your time,
that you never had enough of anyway.
they take up your bed space,
that extra little bit you liked to stretch out in.
they crawl into your heart,
and make it their home,
until, with love, you are insane.
and then they leave.
they leave you wondering
how life was before them,
and how you'll ever fill
all these empty spaces.

writings of you

writing became my addition,
               my passion
she stole my sleep,
demanding to be given words to satiate her.

but it was writing about you,
                    more specifically,
that I was so addicted to.

I wrote of your shy smile,
              your breath on my neck
I wrote of your caress,
             and the way my name tasted off
your lips

I write of you,
I write of you everyday

I write to keep you close,
             because my writings of you
are all I have left to hold on to.

black bedroom

it's sunday and it's gorgeous
and I'm in my black bedroom,
curled at the corner of my bed,
crying and cursing,
because here comes the time
where I leave you.

see you in my dreams

I haven't seen you in months
but you always visit in my dreams.
you wrap your arms around my waist
kiss my neck tenderly as I drift
and whisper your broken promises
one more time into my ear.
but, god, I hate when I start to stir
for when I wake,
the only thing there to greet me
are wet tears on my face.

liar

you said you would do
whatever it took
to be with me

but you lied

kindness never knew us

can I ask you if
you're happy
with the way our lives
turned out?
we met,
and love was there to greet us.
we moved in together,
and faith was there to hold us.
and trust,
god, I gave trust to you,
gave her to you unquestionably.
I gave her so much
it wasn't long before
heartbreak crept in, the
sneaky bitch.
she came because
kindness?
kindness never knew us.

two things

the two things that have
shaped me the most:
meeting you
& losing you

we gave something up

I gave something up
for the sake of this love
because I was 18
because I was young.
you gave up my trust
threw it in the trash
and freely gave away your love.
we gave something up.
we gave something up.
we gave away this love,
as if it meant nothing to us.

a night of no new things

my first night with my new lover –
he said I was his first
but he was not mine.
he kissed my neck,
as you had done so many times.
he touched me there,
a spot that was only yours.
he pressed himself into me,
and I swear I thought I was
still with you.
he is my new lover,
and it was a night of no new things.

the lies I tell you

I know you know
that thing we won't talk about
the elephant in the room
that we tiptoe around
I want you to yell
I want you to shout
I want you to curse and cry
ask me *why?!*
I know you know
that I was with him
you can still smell him on my skin
but you choose to believe
the lies I tell you

and I want you to scream.

the sheets remember you

this bed
far too big for just me
aches without you here.
this pillow
that I laid upon
while you made love to me
just reminds me I now am lonely
these sheets
still smell like you,
as if you're only in the next room
and will be coming back to bed.
but I am alone.
this bed, this pillow,
my lonely.
these sheets ache with your absence;
these sheets remember you.

tumultuous

my always,
we were always tumultuous.
the good came in waves,
the bad came in equally.
we fought, we fought
to keep our heads above the water.
but there were times we almost drowned.
you were almost the death of me
but then you rescued me.
my forever,
I still have water in my lungs
and I can't breathe.

bottom of a bottle

it is friday night
and everyone is out,
drinking away
another week.
but I am tucked,
solitary,
into basement apartment three
discovering how deep
missing you goes
at the bottom
of the bottle
and hoping
you're thinking
of me.

I worry so much about the permanent scar I will have for loving you.

just maybe

we officially ended yesterday. after four tumultuous, yet amazing, years. right now is the most bittersweet feeling in the world. to be single after so long. I've forgotten who I am without you. I'll figure it out, of course. but I really thought when I married, it'd be to you; I really thought I'd lay next to you for the next eighty years; I really thought you loved me enough to change your messed up ways. I really thought you were it. and now I need to face the reality. I need to pick up the pieces. I need to recover and rebuild. I need to learn myself all over again. and I will. and every once in a while, as the snow falls outside, or maybe rain, I'll pour myself a generous glass of wine, look out the window and remember all you were to me. and maybe, just maybe, that will be enough.

the loving or the leaving

the loneliness is so very vast
I didn't know it would feel quite this empty
who will I turn to
when storm clouds come my way?
who will calm
my fluttering heart
when it is all too much?
you were my solace and strength,
but still my weakness
a toxicity I was attracted to.
forever I'll miss
your body against mine
your calming arms
when my own thoughts terrified me.
forever I'll wonder
which piece of you
was my greatest mistake,
the loving or the leaving.

the end

I saw the end
coming from miles away
and we fought it
and we denied it
but it always hovered
there in the distance,
taunting us,
telling us to
enjoy each other now
because we won't get
the forever we planned.
I grieved you while you
were still here with me
and now that you're gone,
I feel nothing, and empty.

used to the silence

please don't let me become used to this silence. please don't become an abstract memory I avoid. the ache in my heart when I wake up to not a single word from you – do you even miss me at all? the desire for it to be you every time the phone rings – but, no, of course it never is. and why would it be? I said goodbye, but you wandered away without any fight. the want in my heart when something happens and I reach for my phone to tell you – but wait, you're not a part of my life anymore. I didn't know silence could sting more than a thousand foul words from your perfect lips. please do not let me become used to this silence – it is so loud I can barely hear myself think.

I know

"you're going to regret this,"
I say as he gets out of my car
for the last time.

"I know."

his honest eyes are breaking my heart.

"so are you,"
he tells me.

I know.

excuse

he tells me
that I made it
very easy
for him
to walk away
and I hear the excuse
all over it.
the truth is
he didn't know
how to stay.

small crimes against you

it is my aim
every day
to sin against you,
small crimes.
an eye roll here,
an exaggerated sigh
so you know I'm
over you,
a sarcastic, biting remark
and picking small fights.
this way
when I commit the
big crimes against you
(when I am
in his bed)
it will not
feel quite so wrong.

all the nameless

her, and her, and her
he confessed
my heart strewn across
the floor and stomped on.
I pictured her on top of you
you between her legs
I do not know these women
but my *hate, hate, hate* for them
burns me alive
as I picture them yelling out
your name in lust
as you yell out theirs
while I hover in the back of your mind,
waiting, for you, at home.

tell me where the hope lives

I chose you over
my family that hated you,
hoping that we could make it work.
I forgave you,
hoping you wouldn't cheat again
with another girl.
I accepted your ring,
hoping it could fix what we had,
what was dying.
but *tell me, tell me*
where the hope lives
so I can gather up some more
because I used it all up on you
and still I want to hope more.

the scary part

you laid beside me
tears streaming down both our faces
you said being without me
would be the scariest part of your life
and you were afraid it was soon.
I clasped your hand
we cried
we kissed
we said *I love you*
we knew
it would be one of the last times.
we knew the end was catching up to us
we couldn't keep out running it,
we are weak and out of breath from trying
and soon our legs will give out.
it will be the scariest part of our lives
and I am cursing everything in the world
because how can we have this much love
and still not each other?

to the one who got away

please know that I still think of you. of your ambition, and the way you inspired me to be a better lover & human. of your wide smile, and the way your eyes danced. of the way you were my friend above all else. how I could talk to you about anything under the sun, and you'd listen.

please know that I still think of your hands on me. of how nervous I was when I first told you I liked you and how you cupped my cheek, pulled me close, and your lips met me halfway. and how you had no clue how to kiss, but we practiced for hours and you got the hang of it.

please don't forget about our time together. how I adored you, how it felt when we kissed. tell me you still think of time we rolled around in hotel sheets, and how you held me for hours.

I still think of how my stomach bottomed out when you said you didn't want anything serious. I still think about how I thought I could change your mind, and I kept you in my life because you breathed the life into me, and you didn't even know. how losing you broke my heart, even though you were never really mine.

to the one who got away, please know there is one thing I always wanted to say: *I love you.* but now, it is simply too late.

I wish you a beautiful life.

about that boy

did I tell you
that you remind me of him
and the reason I've fallen for him
is he reminds me of you

did I tell you
that when the earth starts to warm up again
those first warm days remind me
of his lips on my skin

did I tell you
I fell for him and it was beautiful
and tragic and he never wanted anything serious

did I tell you
about that boy
and how he almost stole me from you
and you remind me of him

sorry

your "sorry"
& my "sorry"
are two different things.
you are sorry you let me down (again)
you are sorry you did exactly what you promised
you wouldn't (again)
& I am sorry that I am even still here,
I am sorry that I even gave you a chance
to be sorry, again.

losing you

the worst part
of losing you
is slowly realizing
my own feelings have changed.
your kiss,
I wish it stirred me like it used to.
I wish we could go back to the beginning.
how did we try so hard,
and yet still our love died?
I want to be head over heels with you again
but I'm not.
the worst part
of losing you
is realizing I want to.

abruptly, intensely

we began
abruptly, intensely.
it scared me
how much I needed you
how much I gave for you.
it scared you
how passionately we loved
how sure we were that this
was the one.
we ended
abruptly, intensely.

the later

falling

I am falling
          falling
wondering
if anyone is
waiting
to catch me
silently
I scream
my eyes
closed
wide
and a
fire
inside

sleeping with the lights on

alone, and on my own
though leaving you had to be done
I miss you in the silent spaces
of an apartment too large for one
and a bed you once kept me safe in
and now I'm sleeping with the lights on
because life without you is so fucking scary

break again

there are days
I feel okay.
days I forget the pain you
caused and the lies I loved
because they
came from your lips.
and there are days
I walk down the street
haunted by each corner
and place we made memories
and I still see your smiling face
leaning in to kiss me
and I break

and I break

and I break

again.

your shirt

your shirt, still on my bed
but the flowers are wilting
and you don't hear my heart
calling out your name
asking you *why, babe?*
why wasn't I enough?
why did you take away your love?
your pictures are still here
that smile and that beautiful laugh,
can I ever get that back?
cause in my head you're still mine
and we're sipping on red wine
you're making love to me all night . . .

your shirt's still on my bed
and we're happy in my head.

when I get where I'm going

this train ride
taking me
miles away
from you
is an attempt
to figure
out the truth
what I'm
looking for
I'm not sure
maybe a
pair of keys
to unlock
a hidden
door
inside will be
a treasure of
secrets
and out my
heart will pour
when I get
where I'm going
I'll come
back to you
we'll make up
for lost time
and I'll tell
you the truth
expect a call
or a letter

in the mail
know I
will find you
I refuse
to fail
every night
I'll sing
to the moon
knowing on
the other side
is you

I have to let you go, again.

thank goodness you've given me so much practice

you will always

you will always
be my epic
once in a lifetime
love of my life
you will forever
be the one
that mattered

let you go (I don't know)

I have to
let you go
let you go
let you go

but how can I
when there is still so much
I don't know?

I don't know
how the neon looks
on your skin
in the early weekend hours

I don't know
how your kiss feels
when the music is so loud
it thrums in our chests

I don't know
how pale you take your coffee
or if you prefer friday
nights or sunday mornings

I don't know
I don't know
I don't know

how can I begin to let you go;
there is still so much of you to learn

when I get where I'm going: another story

my love, I wish you could help
and I know this isn't fair
but I must do this on my own
I will walk this road alone

I'll miss you everyday
and I hope you find your way

but please don't ever change
you're all I need, so stay

when I get where I'm going
I'll give you a call
I'll write a letter to explain it all
then you can make sense of this tragic fall

I wish I didn't have to leave you behind
but what I'm looking for, you cannot find
I wish you could be there by my side
but even I feel the need to hide

I hope

you look

for me

in the

next girl

winter without you

the chill in the air
reminds me of you.
it was cold when I
sacrificed everything
for this love
and we spent all winter
trying to figure out
what the hell we
were doing
but we laughed together,
and we kept each other warm
and we made some semblance
of a happy life, our cheeks
bright red from the cold,
from laughter, from blushing.
the chill in the air
reminds me this winter
I will be so, so cold.

my poetry

when you
who meant
the world to me
stopped reading
my poetry
and about it he
was always asking
well, my love,
what can I say?
all my poems
were about him
after that day.

numb

numb –
as I drive home
wishing that I felt that
heart-wrenching pain,
the stab of betrayal,
a sadness escaping from
my eyes. anything
would be better than
the passive
nothing-ness
I feel as away from
you I finally drive.

"finally"

it took years to get some sense in me – to realize leaving you was leaving everything. if I call you up, will you be waiting for me? tell me on the other end I'll hear you whisper "finally."

amber

you made my name one
that was only
whispered
in conversations
so no one could
catch
my sins
"who's amber?"
they'd ask,
and someone leans close
and whispers
*"she's the girl that left,
and never came back."*

where we hide our wild things

hide the depression
hide the injustice
hide, hide, hide
you're human, girl
flesh and blood
fuck your mental status
we're humans
and we deny it
we hide our wild things
our kinks and flaws
especially our
depressive thoughts
hide the depression
fuck your mental status
hide, hide, hide

legacies of ruin

r u i n
I leave behind
a path in my wake
a heart that loves to ache.
for why else would
I build everything up
just to tear it down
with my own two hands?
and I'll bleed out
from my heart
knowing it never
gets better
because I'm addicted
to legacies of
r u i n

poets
love hard and
love forever

you drift further and further away
in heart and in time and in space
and yet here I am,
our love still filling up all these pages
immortalizing you as a god
this love goes on and on

ready and willing

he is ready and willing
to pick up the broken pieces
of me you left so carelessly
on my bedroom floor.
to put in the time and attention
it will require to put every piece
back in its proper place,
pouring his love into the cracks,
hoping when I am whole again
my heart I can give him.
he is ready and willing
to clean up another man's mess,
and I am in no condition
to stop him.

zookeeper

I went to the zoo
with my love
on a day where we
didn't check the weather forecast
but we were high on life
and mary jane so it didn't matter anyway.
we laughed and giggled our way
through the reptile house,
a reprieve from the rain.
an old zookeeper sat there,
watching his turtles,
all his things packed up
and ready to go home,
but still he stayed and watched them
and I thought maybe they were all he had.
and I thought how sad it was
but at least the turtles had someone who cared.
someone who silently sat with them
through the rain
and I told my love how I wanted that,
for him to silently sit with me
and all my broken pieces
but I don't think he heard me,
and when we left all I felt
was rain.

quiet hours

and in the early quiet hours of the morning
when birds are all I hear,
I sit and miss you
and all the crazy
that loving you entailed.

flowers

you bought me flowers
on the day you left.
through tears you told me
you'd just leave them on
my doorstep.
but they never showed up.
I imagine them on your bed
wilting, fading, dying
as if they imitated
all our mistakes.
how long will you keep
their decaying petals
sleeping next to you
in place of me?
remember what we learned,
love, you can only hold on
for so long.

I may have been too honest with you
but I don't regret it

-you either want all of me or none of me

shattered glass & bruised ego

be careful, love
do not cut yourself
on the shattered glass
of my aching heart.
be careful, love
my bruised ego
can't take much more,
it's been hurt
too many times before.

what we will be

you know
that I know
what you want to be to me.
I know
that you know
what I want to do to you.
let's wait, babe.
let's enjoy every second
as we anticipate
all the things we'll be,
as we cat and mouse
each other pretending
not to flirt, but we know
what we will do
to each other.

*-you will protect my heart and I will ravage
your body*

almost

when you sailed
on the lake
did you think of my eyes –
did you *almost*?

the way we *almost* had the right timing
the way we *almost* felt the same way
the way we *almost* had it all
the way I think I'm *almost* over you

except –

I'm not
I'm not
I'm not
even close

if I could unpart my thighs

I saved it,
while every girl
threw it in the trash
like it didn't matter.
I saved it,
because only one guy
was worth it.
on my wedding day,
I'd truthfully wear white.
but then I met you.
and I was 18
and my heart melted at your smile
and my body offered itself up willingly.
it hurt so good,
just like the next
three years with you.
but baby,
if I could unpart my thighs,
I might, and
I may have never known you.

s h a t t e r e d

I think of

all the times
you

s h a t t e r e d

my heart
and I swept
all the pieces
up neatly
and gave them
back to you.

I think I
should have
saved a few
small pieces
for myself.

what we reap

the things we reap
ugly scars we keep
mistakes that follow
since the day we turned 18.
you can count
on regrets in this life
oh god, I didn't realize
you'd be my number one
mistake,
your consequences
following me around forever,
ugly scars I keep
the things I reap.

chicago

it is 3 degrees
          in chicago
          so it feels like
          negative fifteen
          and the coldness
          s e e p s
          into my
          blood & bones
          and my toes are numb.
          the coldness can
          choke me,
          I will not fight it.
          even if I made
          it home,
          you would not
          be there
          to warm me.

delicate desire

I think of you in hushed tones
and I try not to think of you too much
I don't say your name in conversation
even though you're right at the tip of my tongue
I will protect this love
this delicate desire
of what we could become
so that we could have a fighting chance
so that you are not another lesson learned,
another chapter in my book,
another 3 a.m. drunk phone call,
another him.

he broke me

he broke me
and I am sorry
that I let you
fall for me
while thinking
I was
whole

-he took pieces of me I will never get back

things that remind me of cristian

1. pizza hut

2. spring

3. the cindy lyn motel

4. white hyundai's

5. homemade margaritas

6. the theater in the quarry

7. *friends* (always, but especially your favorite episode)

8. hershey's kisses

9. feeling my heart split in two

10. wanting m o r e

indian summer

it's mid-november
in chicago
and it's 70 degrees
can you believe it?

I saw you across the street
wearing the same blue shorts
you wore to my apartment in
warm july

my heart jumped to my throat
every fiber of my being
calling out to you
I haven't even begun to let you go

but I did walk away
can you believe it?

you are at the heart
of every bad decision
I have ever made.

I'm scared to start choosing better,
for you will not be there.

trees

they say
you should be your own person
you should be okay being single
a l o n e

but you watched me grow into a woman
for five years and
you loved *every single version of me*

we are trees
and my roots
my branches
are still all tangled up in yours.

after you

after you,
I am more
protective with my heart
now that I know
what giving it away can do.

-it still hasn't healed properly

ready for love

you tell me you are not
ready for love,
but you are ready to make it.

-it's so much better when you're in love

winter chills

it is chilly mornings
foggy windows
leaves leaving their
youthful green behind
that reminds me of you.
maybe because all
those years ago,
it was mid-november
when I made that
fateful decision.
I left for you,
and made love to you
atop the blankets.
we moved all my
belongings into your
basement, and pretended
we were old enough to know
what the hell we were doing.
I loved you then,
and I love you more now,
but it's so, so different.
(how do two people stay in love
after they have put each other
through what we have?)
and when the air warms,
the earth comes back to life and
tulips bloom,

I wish, I wish
it was you I was thinking of.
but I think of him,
and how he brought me back to life
after your winter chills.

consumed

you have consumed
every last piece of me,
tangled up inside me
leaking into my veins
and making your home
in the center of my tummy.
tell me, was I tasty?

if you are thinking what I am thinking

don't play with me, my love
my life has already been too hard,
too filled with guesses and games
and I am so, so tired of it.
if you are thinking what I am thinking,
then come, come closer.
I will whisper in your ear and
tell you all my secrets and maybe,
just maybe, you'd be willing to
heal all these cracks.
but if you are not thinking what I am thinking,
please stay far, far away from me.
my heart is worn out, exhausted
by lies and disappointments.
it needs tender care and rest.
will you give me that kind of love, love?

there is life after you.

there has to be.

another you

it will never be enough. you were my once in a lifetime, worth risking family and friends and life. I will spend the rest of my life looking for someone whose lips are as sweet as tender as demanding. who knows just how far to let me go before I need to be pulled back into safety. who balances me out and who makes loving me look so effortless even though I know the effort it takes to deal with my mood swings and anxiety and laughter. I will spend the rest of my life looking for another you, and I know I will never find him.

I don't regret it.
we were beautiful while we burned.

-touching you was fireworks

first love

first love is always too strong
for its own good.
it is ridiculous to think
there could ever be
a lover as good as you.

misery riot

the misery is rioting
inside me
and it's
chaos
but I rip apart
a life that
brings no pleasure
and I will rebuild
with this
pain.

this is the part

this is the part where it gets hard;
this is the part where life begins.

how are you doing?

                    aside from the fact that I'm
                          unbelievably numb?

I'm fine, thanks.

maybe you knew

maybe you knew
that I was feeling lost
that I was struggling
and hating
maybe you knew
how many times a day
suicide crossed my mind
but you stood by
watched me self-destruct
rip down every remaining
wall in my life
unit I even ripped down us
maybe you knew
you were the last straw
and you walked away
anyway

planted in pain

I am planted in pain
firmly
a would-be
martyr to these
feelings
I cannot move
I've already put down
these roots
I wallow in such
misery
and I haven't decided
if I will
wither
or bloom

sometimes

I forget which parts of myself
I took from you

and which parts were always mine.

poems are funny to me.
they are blood. sweat. tears.
painful thoughts warring with my mind.
stabs to my heart.
roiling anger. heartbreak.
mixed with all the pretty things.
but here they are. black & white.
simple. neat.
words on a paper.
easy to read.

dreaming

perhaps
all I am good at
is *dreaming*.

forgive me,
it just breaks my heart
how quickly we settle
into suffocating
existences.

my body has run out of tears for you

there isn't room in my heart for you anymore
you've long outstayed your welcome

every shade

we were every shade
of tragic
you could possibly
imagine.
but thank you
for giving me
these words
these thoughts
this book
this beauty.
it is every shade
of you & me.

breathless

breathless
I realize that it
can no longer
be you.

it has to be me.

clean

I am washing you
off my body
for the last time
watching all your
pretty colors
swirl down the drain
the water taking
you further and
further away from me,
and the closest
you'll ever be
to me again.

my heart is filling up again
and I am regaining my smile

and it has nothing to do with you

just write

write, just write.
don't care if it's good
or if a lot of people will "like" it.
care that it is healing your soul.
care that it is your therapy,
that you have all these emotions
piling up on top of one another
and you have to let them out,
let them leak all over the paper
all the good, all the ugly
because this is all of you
baby girl, and you have
to learn how to heal yourself.
just write.

be the love of your own life

the thing about lovers is they don't always grow with you. they stay stuck in their ways and watch you outgrow them.

the thing about lovers is they can become toxic, and you stay and stay and stay because the highs are so, so high. but eventually you can't stay anymore. the thing about lovers is sometimes they break you.

the thing about lovers is sometimes you love them more than they love you. and you'll wonder why you aren't enough for them, why all the love you pour into them just isn't enough.

the thing about lovers is sometimes they'll teach you about yourself and what you want and deserve more than you ever thought possible. more than you ever bargained for. and you'll learn that you have to love yourself first. always.

the thing about lovers is you'll learn to be the love of your own life. anyone else is just along to watch your beautiful ride.

acknowledgements

to my mom and dad – thank you for being the best that you could be for me and morgan. I love you.

to my sister – you are literally my favorite person in the world. thank you for being unapologetically yourself and challenging me to be better.

to ambyr – thank you for the encouragement. I am so blessed to have had you in my life for nearly 20 years. thank you for loving me through it all.

to taylor – thank you for writing down your teenage girl feelings and showing people they are just as valid as everyone else's. it meant the world to my 2006, 11-year-old self and it inspired me to keep writing my feelings. thank you for letting me grow up with you and being my life's soundtrack.

to the boys who broke my heart – thank you for the lessons. thank you for the poetry inspiration. thank you for forcing me to grow. I still wish you all the best.

to my readers – thank you for being here. you are so, so loved.

xoxo,

amber

about the author

amber powers is a twenty-something hopeless romantic who has been writing poetry for as long as she can remember. she lives in the suburbs of chicago with her family and two cats, indy and smokey. *the thing about lovers* is her first poetry collection and was written over the span of a decade.

instagram & tiktok: @powerspoetry